HAI
The Frog

and the Littlest Shaman

EPI PUBLISHING

Deep in the green and humid rain forest of the Amazon sat a small, thatched hut. Outside the hut, children laughed and chased after green lizards, while two women sat in the shade and peeled cassava roots to make flour. The hut was special. It belonged to the village shaman, or medicine man. Shamans are very wise. They know how to use plants to make many different medicines, and their knowledge can help to treat sick people all over the world.

From inside that special hut, came a CRASH! The women looked at each other and smiled. "Not again!" said one.

Inside the hut a small boy named Kiwen was picking up the scattered pieces of the broken pot. "Sorry, Paho" said Kiwen, using the native word for "father." Kiwen could feel his face get hot, for this was the third pot he had dropped that day. He was helping his father make medicine from go-lo-be sap, to treat his friend Wayana's earache.

Kiwen's father was a very powerful shaman. Once, an important tribal chief was stung by a wasp and almost died. Kiwen's father had healed him with plant medicines and special prayers. Now Kiwen was learning about plant medicine so that someday he, too, could be a powerful shaman. But Kiwen was very small and he often had trouble reaching the jars that his father had stacked high.

"Maybe he is too small for such important work," grumbled Wayana, who was cranky because of his earache. "He is so small, like a peanut."

Kiwen's face got hot again. This time he almost felt like crying. The shaman started to speak to his son, but it was too late, for Kiwen was already running out the door.

Kiwen's mother and sister stopped peeling cassava and called out to him. "Come back, little one, don't give up so easily!"

Some bigger boys carrying fishing spears passed by and laughed. "Yes, little one, come back here!"

"Little one! Everyone thinks I am a joke! How will I ever be a powerful shaman like my father?" wondered Kiwen as he ran from the sunny village into the dark, thick forest.

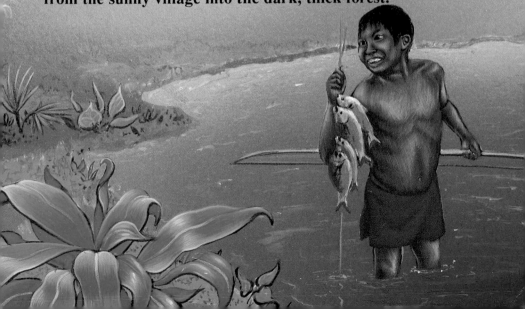

The forest was like a magic cure for Kiwen. It always made him feel better. He wandered under the tall cashew and po-no trees, past spotted snakewood trees and twisting, woody liana vines. A peccary rustled among the dark green ko-noy-uh bushes. Overhead, a red-throated caracara hawk cawed and watched Kiwen crack open and eat a tasty sho nut.

Kiwen found his favorite tree, tall and strong, and climbed up higher than he ever had. He sat on a strong branch near a bromeliad. The bromeliad looked like the top of a pineapple, and inside were cup-shaped areas filled with water. "That would be a good place for a small, unimportant creature like me to crawl in and hide," thought Kiwen.

Kiwen closed his eyes and daydreamed. Sitting still, he imagined what it would be like to climb into the green bromeliad funnel, to peek out at the world, at a little boy sitting on a branch who looks just like . . . Kiwen.

"Oh!" Kiwen opened his eyes and looked into the tiny eyes of a poison dart frog, nested in the bromeliad, watching Kiwen. He was surprised. The frog hadn't been there a moment before! Kiwen knew he shouldn't touch the colorful poison dart frog, because some of them are very poisonous. So he just calmly watched it.

The frog seemed very tranquil; Kiwen felt more peaceful - even sleepy - just looking at it. As he sat quietly and stared at the little frog, a soft voice inside him said "*haito*" which means "content."

"Who said that?" thought Kiwen. "Did I think it?" Then he remembered a story that his father had told him. Like many shamans, his father had an animal spirit guide, which came to him in a dream. His father's spirit guide was a panther, and the panther came to his father's dreams to teach him important lessons.

"Maybe this peaceful little frog is my spirit guide!" thought Kiwen with excitement. "I'll call him Haito. What can you teach me, Haito?"

Kiwen closed his eyes and made his mind quiet. He heard the parrots in the trees, the gurgle of a nearby stream. Then he thought about poison dart frogs. One little frog can make a person very sick! But the frog also makes a substance that can be used as a painkiller. That is very useful to sick people.

"This frog may be little," thought Kiwen, "but it is powerful and important and it doesn't have to hide in a bromeliad. And neither do I."

"Thank you, Haito," said Kiwen as he opened his eyes. "Your lesson is good." He stopped. Haito was gone! Kiwen looked all around, but there was no sign of the little frog.

As he climbed back down the tree, Kiwen wondered if the frog was ever really there. Yet somehow he knew that he would see it again. "Here in my favorite tree, we will meet again, spirit guide," said Kiwen. "And please visit me in my dreams." As he spoke, the caracara hawk cocked its head at him in curiosity.

Kiwen walked tall as he strode through the green magic of the forest, bound for home. As he passed some go-lo-be mushrooms, he remembered the jar of sap he had broken this morning. Kiwen picked as much as he could carry, and continued steadily toward the village.

The late afternoon light touched Kiwen's village with gold as he walked slowly and proudly toward his father's hut. The bigger boys, who had just returned from fishing, said nothing as Kiwen passed them. His mother, baking bread with the cassava dough, said, "That's a fine bunch of go-lo-bo you've picked, Kiwen."

Kiwen entered the shaman's hut and stood before his father. "Paho, I am sorry I ran away before. It won't happen again. I will stay and learn no matter what, and become a great shaman like you are," he said. "And I picked go-lo-be to replace what I spilled."

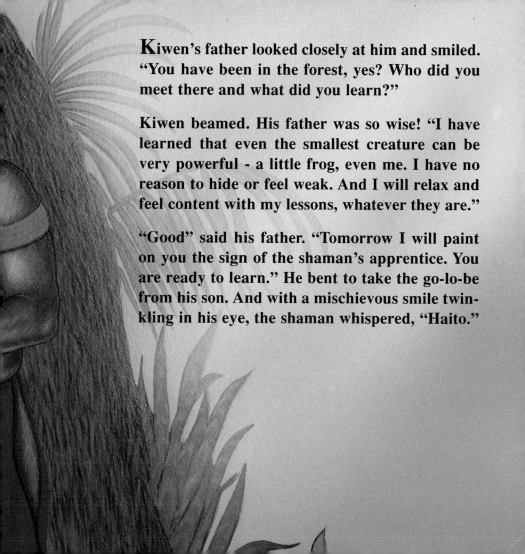

Kiwen's father looked closely at him and smiled. "You have been in the forest, yes? Who did you meet there and what did you learn?"

Kiwen beamed. His father was so wise! "I have learned that even the smallest creature can be very powerful - a little frog, even me. I have no reason to hide or feel weak. And I will relax and feel content with my lessons, whatever they are."

"Good" said his father. "Tomorrow I will paint on you the sign of the shaman's apprentice. You are ready to learn." He bent to take the go-lo-be from his son. And with a mischievous smile twinkling in his eye, the shaman whispered, "Haito."

Kiwen is a very small boy with a very strong and respected father. With Haito's help, he learned to respect himself and find his own importance in the world. This made him relaxed and content. Someday Kiwen, too, will be a respected shaman.